Crunchy Christmas Murder

Book Four

in

Killer Cookie

Cozy Mysteries

By

Patti Benning

Author's Note: On the next page, you'll find out how to access all of my books easily, as well as locate books by best-selling author, Summer Prescott. I'd love to hear your thoughts on my books, the storylines, and anything else that you'd like to comment on – reader feedback is very important to me. Please see the following page for my publisher's contact information. If you'd like to be on her list of "folks to contact" with updates, release and sales notifications, etc…just shoot her an email and let her know. Thanks for reading!

Also…

…if you're looking for more great reads, from me and Summer, check out the Summer Prescott Publishing Book Catalog:

http://summerprescottbooks.com/book-catalog/ for some truly delicious stories.

Contact Info for Summer Prescott Publishing:

Twitter: @summerprescott1

Blog and Book Catalog: http://summerprescottbooks.com

Email: summer.prescott.cozies@gmail.com

And...look up The Summer Prescott Fan Page on Facebook – let's be friends!

If you're an author and are interested in publishing with Summer Prescott Books – please send Summer an email and she'll send you submission guidelines.

TABLE OF CONTENTS

CHAPTER ONE.. 10

CHAPTER TWO.. 19

CHAPTER THREE... 28

CHAPTER FOUR 37

CHAPTER FIVE 45

CHAPTER SIX 52

CHAPTER SEVEN 60

CHAPTER EIGHT.. 68

CHAPTER NINE 73

CHAPTER TEN.. 79

CHAPTER ELEVEN 85

CHAPTER TWELVE 91

CHAPTER THIRTEEN 96

CHAPTER FOURTEEN 103

CHAPTER FIFTEEN.. 109

CHAPTER SIXTEEN 119

CRUNCHY CHRISTMAS
MURDER

Book Four in Killer Cookie Cozy Mysteries

CHAPTER ONE

L ilah Fallon signed her name on the final line with a flourish and put the pen down. She gazed at her signature, then looked across the table to the real estate agent.

"What now?" she asked. Her heart pounding as if she had just run a mile instead of scribbling her name at the bottom of a few pages.

"We'll review everything, and plan on closing in a couple of days," the agent said. She was a younger woman, with a brusque and businesslike manner. "If nothing comes up, you will be able to pick up the keys on Friday."

"Thank you so much," Lilah said. "Should I wait for your call, or check in tomorrow and see how things are going?"

"I'll give you a call to set up a time and place to meet to hand over the keys." She stood up, sliding the papers into her briefcase and snapping it firmly shut before straightening her shirt. "Is there anything else you have questions about?"

"No, I don't think so," Lilah said, trying to straighten out her thoughts. It was hard to focus on anything other than the fact that she had just signed off on the building that would eventually become her very own cookie shop.

"If there's nothing else, expect my call before Thursday. Have a nice evening."

The real estate agent left the coffee shop, tossing her empty cup in the garbage bin on the way out. Lilah sat in her seat for a few minutes longer, drinking the rest of her own espresso while she let it sink in. She had bought the store. This was really happening. It was a big step — huge — and a little bit terrifying. There was a lot on the line for this cookie shop, and she wasn't the only one who had taken a risk. One of her closest friends, Margie Hatch, had loaned her the money to get started, and she was determined to pay her back as soon as possible.

"Lilah Fallon, small business owner," she said to herself, trying it out. It sounded a lot better to her ears than Lilah Fallon, waitress. Not that she minded her job at the diner. In fact, she enjoyed it quite a lot. It just wasn't what she wanted to do for the rest of her life.

If she was being honest with herself, she wasn't quite sure that owning a cookie shop was what she wanted to do for the rest of her life, either. She *thought* it was, but then just a few months ago, she had thought being a hair stylist was her ideal career. She already knew that she enjoyed baking, but what about the business side of it all? Would it be as stressful and fast paced as her job at her father's company had been? She didn't want to get burned out again after a few years.

"Where is all this worrying coming from?" she said aloud, trying to snap herself out of the anxiety that had suddenly gripped her. "This is what I want to do with my life for now, and if I change my mind twenty years down the road, well, that isn't the end of the world."

She got up and dumped the empty coffee cup in the trash before shrugging on her light jacket and shouldering her purse. She could worry later. Right now, it was time to celebrate.

Margie Hatch was not only her friend and business partner, but also her neighbor. Lilah had had no idea how lucky she was getting when she rented the little yellow house a couple of years ago when she had first moved to the small town of Vista, Alabama. Margie had been there for her through so much, that Lilah sometimes wondered where she would be without her.

She pulled the car into her gravel driveway and looked fondly at the little house. It wasn't much; one bedroom, a bathroom, a kitchen, a breakfast nook, and a living room, with no basement or garage, but she didn't mind. It was a cozy house, and had everything she needed to feel at home.

Sitting in the windowsill watching her was an orange tabby cat. Oscar had been with her for six years; she had adopted him from the pound when he was just a little kitten. He always greeted her at the door, along with her beagle, Winnie. She knew that she would have to go in and say a quick hello to them before she walked over to Margie's house; Oscar would never forgive her if she ignored him.

One of the things that she had always loved about her friend's house was the warm, vanilla scent that her kitchen had soaked up from decades of baking. For the first time, she noticed a similar scent in her own kitchen when she walked through the door. It was one of the many subtle signs of how much her life had gradually changed over the years, and it filled her with happiness.

"Hey, you two," she said as the dog and cat came around the corner to greet her. She fished a pair of treats out of the owl-shaped cookie jar on the counter for them, then bent down to give each a quick pet. They wouldn't be happy when she left again so quickly, but she wouldn't be far, and she planned to spend some quality time on the couch with them this evening with a glass of wine and a good movie.

She changed quickly into something more comfortable, and left just a few minutes later, heading across her yard to Margie's house. Her friend pulled the door open as she walked up the porch steps.

"I saw you pull in," the older woman explained. "How did it go?"

"I signed," Lilah replied, a grin spreading across her face. "I should have the keys by Thursday."

"Oh, Lilah." Margie wrapped her in a hug, her own face split into a happy smile. "I'm so happy for you."

"It hardly feels real. I'm still in shock. After everything that happened over the past few weeks, I didn't think I would end up being able to get that place."

The old sandwich shop that Lilah had fallen so in love with had gotten tied up in a fatal family feud shortly after it first came on the market. Knowing that it might be a long time before things got settled, she had looked at a few other buildings around town, but none of them had felt as right as the little sandwich shop on Main Street. She still felt a shiver of disbelieving joy when she remembered getting the call from the real estate agent, telling her that the shop was back on the market.

"How is everything else going?" Margie asked as the two of them walked into the house together.

Lilah knew that she was asking about the rest of the many small tasks that had to be done before she could open the doors of the cookie shop for the first time. The amount of work that went into opening even a small business with no employees was astounding.

"Well, I finished registering as an LLC, and I've got the identification number that I'll need for taxes. All that's really left to do is to get the kitchen inspected, but that has to wait until everything is set up," she told her friend. "The shop should be able to open by Christmas, as long as nothing else comes up."

The two women chatted for another few minutes as they worked on lunch together. Lilah had a feeling that the older woman appreciated having company in the kitchen almost as much as Lilah appreciated the good, home cooked meal that was the result. Her son, daughter in law, and three grandchildren had left not long after Thanksgiving, and the older woman's house had seemed unusually quiet since then.

Lunch was baked chicken breasts with a creamy Alfredo sauce, topped with bacon bits and fresh Parmesan cheese. Lilah was put in charge of the salad, and as she rinsed off the organic lettuce in the sink, her mind wandered helplessly. She didn't even have the keys yet, but she was already coming up with designs and color schemes for the cookie shop. She would run everything by Margie first, of course. She wanted her friend to be as involved in the store as possible. After all, she was the one that had made all of this possible...

"Lilah, dear, you usually only have to pump that three or four times."

Her friend's voice interrupted her thoughts, and she looked down to realize that she had been drying the lettuce in the salad spinner for far longer than was necessary. Embarrassed, she let the contraption spin to a stop before taking out the leaves.

"Sorry," she said. "I'm just too excited. I don't know how I'm going to make it until Thursday. I'm going to be so scatterbrained at work this afternoon; I'll probably forget to turn the fryer off and burn the diner down."

"Oh, Randall has insurance on that thing through the roof. He'd probably thank you if you did."

Laughing, Lilah returned to the salad that she was supposed to be making. She tried to push her excitement — and apprehension — to the back of her mind for the time being. Thursday would come soon enough, and once she got the keys she would be lucky to have even a few moments of free time between all of the renovations and inspections that would have to be done before the shop could finally open. She wanted to do her best to appreciate these last few days before she took the plunge into the world of being a small business owner.

CHAPTER TWO

"Two eggs sunny side up, bacon, and hash browns," Lilah said, setting the plate down in front of her customer. "Is there anything else I can get you?"

"Just a coffee refill. Thanks." The man was a burly trucker from out of state; a common type of customer at the little diner, which was located just off of the state highway. Vista was a small town, but it got a lot of through traffic, which formed most of the diner's customer base. That was another reason why she was so glad that she had been able to buy the old sandwich shop; its location on Main Street was just perfect.

"I'll be right back with that," she told him, offering him a bright smile that she hoped would earn her an extra couple of dollars on the tip.

It was Thursday, and in just three hours she had her meeting with the real estate agent to pick up the keys to the sandwich shop. Time seemed to be inching by painfully slowly that morning; no matter how long she made herself wait before glancing at the clock, only a few minutes would have passed. Still, she was glad to be able to spend the morning working instead of waiting at home. She had never been the patient type. At least an extra shift at the diner gave her something to do besides pace and check her phone for updates every couple of seconds.

After refilling her customer's coffee, she returned to the kitchen where Randall was cooking an omelet for his own late breakfast. Randall Price was the diner's owner, and only full time cook. He worked at the restaurant seven days a week, and had only been gone a handful of times in the years that Lilah had worked there.

"Do you have a final day for me yet?" he asked without looking at her, his eyes focused on his omelet as he carefully folded it in half.

"Not yet," she said, taking a seat at one of the ancient bar stools along the back wall. "I'll be able to give you an answer after the cookie shop has been open for a week or two."

"You aren't usually this cautious," he said, maneuvering the overstuffed omelet onto a plate. "I can't count the number of times you've quit here for a new job just minutes after you got hired."

He didn't mention all of the times she had returned, begging for her job back, just weeks later, for which she was grateful. "This just feels... different. I want to make sure I'm doing things right," she said.

"Maybe this time it's different because you're treating it differently," he suggested slyly. "You have more control over your life than you think, Lilah."

She was still trying to figure out a good answer to that when she heard the jingle from the front doors that announced another customer had come in for brunch. Leaving Russell, to enjoy his omelet in peace, she pushed through the swinging door between the kitchen and the dining area to find her best friend, Valerie Palmer, waiting to be seated. She didn't recognize the woman standing next to her, but gave her a friendly nod anyway.

"Hey, Val," she said as she grabbed two menus from behind the counter. "Do you two need a booth, or do you just want to sit at the counter?"

"We'll take a booth," her friend said. "Can you join us? I told Lydia about your cookie shop, and she wants to hear more. Her sister runs a similar shop in Montgomery; maybe you could call her and get some pointers."

"Lydia Lopez," the other woman said, shaking Lilah's hand. "My sister, Brigette, has a wonderful little store called Daydream Cookies and Cakes. She's doing pretty well for herself, and would be happy to share her story with someone like you."

"I'd love to chat," Lilah said. "Let's sit at the booth in the corner. I'll get your drink orders, then pop into the kitchen to tell Randall I'm taking my break. We aren't that busy right now, so I don't think he'll mind."

A few minutes later the three of them were sitting at the booth, chatting together like old friends. A visit from Val turned out to be just what Lilah needed. Hearing about Lydia's sister and her journey from being someone brand new to the business world to a successful store owner made the time go by more quickly, and helped Lilah feel more confident that what she was doing was right.

"Here, I'll give you Brigette's business card," Lydia said. "I'll give her a call tonight and tell her about you. I think the two of you will hit it off. If you need help finding suppliers or anything, she's your gal."

"Thanks," Lilah said. She slid the card into her pocket, making a mental note to enter the woman's contact information into her phone before she lost it. "So, what do you do, Lydia?"

"Nothing as impressive as running a business," the other woman said with a laugh. "I work part time at the florist. My husband, John, works at the machine shop and supports the both of us." Lydia's face fell. "That might change soon, though."

"What?" Val said, putting down her soda and turning to look at her friend. "What happened?"

"He might get laid off," Lydia said.

"I didn't know that," Val replied. "I'm sorry. I thought the factory was doing well?"

"It is; so well that they're going to be getting a new machine that can do his job more quickly and more efficiently than he can." She sighed and spun her glass slowly on the table. "I just heard about it an hour ago. He came home from work early, and was in a terrible mood. It turns out that he found out today that his boss, Mr. Townsend, was planning on letting a bunch of people go a few weeks after Christmas. I guess he saw a letter lying open on a desk, something that he wasn't supposed to see. He didn't really want to talk about it much, so I left him alone to cool down."

"Wait — Mr. Townsend... you mean Reid?" Lilah interrupted.

"Reid Townsend, yes," Lydia said. "Why? Do you know him?"

Lilah and Val traded a glance. She knew him, all right. He was friends with both Margie and Val, and had even grown up in the same house that Lilah was renting now. He asked her out occasionally, though she always said no. His life was too fast paced and business oriented for her, but despite that she had come to see that he was a good guy at heart. She couldn't imagine him laying off his men without good reason.

"I do," she replied at last. "He's an acquaintance. I'm sorry about your husband. At least the two of you have more of a head's up though, right?"

Lydia shrugged. "I'm sure John will come around and look at it that way eventually. He's still fuming right now. Apparently, he and his boss got into a major argument about it — it almost came to blows, from what he said."

"Wow." Val let out a low whistle. "It sounds like there was plenty of drama at the machine shop this morning."

"That's not even all of it. John has… well, he has some issues with keeping his temper under control. I guess one of the other guys heard the argument getting heated and called the police. I don't blame them, with John's reputation, but I don't think he'll ever get over it. Now he's mad, worried about losing the job next month, and embarrassed about getting sent home early."

"Yikes," Lilah said. "Will the two of you be all right, though? I've never been laid off, but I definitely know what it's like to have to scramble to make ends meet."

"We'll be fine. I can switch to full time at the florist and start doing deliveries. It'll bring in enough money to support us until he finds another job." She laughed dryly. "Who knows, maybe John will drink himself into oblivion before all of this is over, and his life insurance will kick in."

Lilah traded another look with Val. Seeing their expression, Lydia quickly added, "I'm just kidding, of course. I love the guy, even if he drives me up the wall sometimes."

"My fiancé drives me bonkers sometimes, too," Val said. "I'm sure I do the same to him, though."

As the conversation moved to the topic of significant others, Lilah's eyes wandered over to the clock. Spending time chatting with the two women had made time pass surprisingly quickly. The minute hand seemed to have jumped forward. In no time at all, she would be clocking out and on her way to go pick up the keys to the sandwich shop. In just over an hour, the next big journey of her life would begin.

CHAPTER THREE

The deadbolt gave a satisfying thunk as Lilah turned the key in the door for the first time. The last time she had been inside the sandwich shop, she had been attacked by a killer, but she felt safe in the knowledge that the woman responsible was now in prison. She didn't feel any trepidation as she pushed the door open to the dark, silent kitchen, only excitement. It was hard to believe that the place was really hers now. Everything was final, and the entire process had gone smoothly from start to finish. It felt like a dream.

With everything shut off to conserve power, the only light in the kitchen was coming in through the small windows up near the ceiling. The room looked peaceful, and Lilah enjoyed the quiet for a moment while she shut the door behind her and put her purse down on the table. When she found the light switch panel on the back wall, it took her a couple of tries to find the right set of switches for the kitchen. When the room was flooded with light at last, it looked bright and cheery; just what she would want for the long hours she planned on spending back here to make cookies.

The walk-in fridge and freezer had been shut off and left open to air out while the building was unoccupied. They both looked clean, but she wanted to give them a once over before turning them back on. She would have to test all of the appliances thoroughly before she spent any of the extra money she had set aside on decorating. It wouldn't do her much good to have newly painted walls and a custom sign if the oven ended up breaking down when she fired it up to make her first batch of cookies.

Trying not to feel daunted by the enormity of the task in front of her, she took one last look around the kitchen, then went back out to her car to bring in the cleaning supplies and necessities, such as toilet paper and bottled water, that she had prepared for the big day. She had clocked out of the diner a few hours ago; now it was time to really get to work.

"Not bad," Lilah said to herself. She was standing with her hands on her hips, looking around herself with satisfaction. The freezer and walk in fridge were both humming quietly in the background. She would check the temperatures tomorrow to make sure they were both within the guidelines that she had pulled off of the internet. She was determined to pass the inspection the first time around, and didn't want to miss a thing.

The oven and stove top had both been scrubbed and scraped clean and tested, and she had swept out the large pantry after putting a new light bulb in the fixture. She had just finished wiping down the counters, cleaning the sinks, and mopping the floor. She was finally satisfied that the kitchen was clean enough to cook in. Tomorrow, she planned on bringing some ingredients from home to cook the first ever batch of cookies in her new store.

With the most important room cleaned up, she decided to take a short break and grab a cup of hot soup from the deli on the corner. It was easy walking distance from the store, and she had the feeling that she would be making a lot of trips for soup and coffee during the long hours that she planned on spending at the cookie shop. She wasn't planning on hiring any employees until she was confident that the cookie shop would be a success. For one, hiring someone else would just make everything more complicated when it came to finances. Besides that, she didn't even know if the little shop would bring in enough money to support her, let alone a second or third person.

It was certainly an uncertain path she was taking. She could only hope that things would keep going her way in the years to come. She knew that no matter how well she planned and budgeted, the fate of her shop would ultimately rest in the hands of luck. All she could do was put her best effort forward and hope.

She brought the soup back to the sandwich shop — she wouldn't feel right calling it a cookie shop until she had made the first batch of cookies — and settled down at the rickety old table in the front room that had been left behind by the previous owner. The front of the shop had a huge display window that took up most of the front wall. It would be perfect for cookie displays. She made a mental note to do something up for the holidays, but for now she settled with watching the passersby as they went about their business on Main Street as she ate.

When she had put her empty soup container in the trash bag, she went on to her next task; finalizing the colors she wanted to paint the cookie shop. Ever since she had first seen the sandwich shop, she had been fantasizing about the interior decorating. So much could be achieved with just paint and stencils. The only problem was settling on an idea. She didn't want to regret her choice a week, a month, or even a year later. She had borrowed an entire book of sample colors from the local hardware store, and was planning on going through it for the rest of her evening at the store.

It wasn't until the sun began to set and the natural light began to fade that Lilah put the book down and rubbed her eyes, realizing that it was past dinner time for Oscar and Winnie. The poor things were probably wondering where she was; it was time to get going. She was pretty sure that she had made her final choice for the cookie shop's color scheme, but wanted to sleep on it before purchasing the paint and locking herself in to a decision. She had spent enough time in the little shop for the evening. It was time to get home and get some rest before tackling the next big project.

"I'm sorry I was gone so long, you two."

Lilah slipped through her front door and nudged her way past the eager cat and dog in an attempt to put some of her stuff down before petting them. Winnie wasn't having any of that, and jumped up, barking happily. A couple of treats from the owl cookie jar bought her just enough time to put her purse and the paint color sample book down and take off her shoes before the dog needed attention again.

After she let the beagle outside to do her thing, Lilah followed the meowing Oscar to the end table where his food bowl was. She grabbed the bag of kibble from a high shelf and gave him a scoop, with a little extra as an apology for being so late. Once Winnie was let back inside, she filled her bowl as well.

Seeing her pets happily eating made her smile. She loved both of them, and hoped that this new chapter in their lives together would still leave her plenty of time to spend with them. She would be working two jobs for a while, at least until the cookie shop took off, which would probably mean a lot of late nights and early mornings. They would make it work, though. She would make sure of it. The dog and cat were like family to her, and she would make time for them even if it meant rearranging her schedule.

Feeling content, and just a little bit tired as the long day started to catch up with her, Lilah settled down at the kitchen table with a mug of peppermint hot cocoa and her laptop. She needed to write an email to her mom to tell her about her first day getting the sandwich shop ready, and she also needed to save some more recipes for different kinds of cookies. She hoped to get the shop open before Christmas, which meant that she would need some holiday themed cookies to offer her customers.

She opened up her email and began typing, pausing occasionally to think about what she wanted to say. When she had first told her parents about her plans for the cookie shop, neither of them had been thrilled. Her mother had finally started to share in some of her excitement, but her father was taking longer to come around. She knew that he was hurt that she had left her comfortable job at his company, only to try to start her own business just a couple of years later. A baked goods shop was a far cry from the fast-paced corporate environment that she had left behind, but he just didn't seem to see that.

Lilah finished up the email to her mother, covering all of the best points of the day and trying to convey her excitement and hope for the future. This was a huge step for her, and she wanted her parents to be able to share her optimism. She knew it would take time, but she was sure that one day even her father would come around.

After sending the email, she surfed the internet for a few minutes, checking a couple of websites that made custom signs. All of them had a waiting period of a few weeks, which was longer than she wanted. She knew that she shouldn't have waited for so long to settle on a name, but she had wanted to wait until she had come up with one that felt just right. Now she was really going to have to crunch to get a sign made in time for the grand opening.

Deciding to check out the local glass sketching shop tomorrow, she clicked out of the web page and pulled up a news site, hoping that it wouldn't be too chilly out. When she saw that the temperature would be in the sixties, she smiled. At least she would be able to prop the door open while she painted without freezing. She would have to remember to bring a fan from home to help air the paint fumes out.

She was about to close the browser when a news story caught her eye. *Local Man Found Dead in Pool.* Frowning, she clicked to expand it. What she read made her stomach drop.

John Lopez, 42, was found dead in his swimming pool this afternoon. The police have refused to comment on the cause of death. Earlier this morning, Mr. Lopez had an encounter with the police after a concerned coworker witnessed an emotional outburst on the job. It is unknown at this time whether the two incidents are related.

"Oh my goodness," Lilah whispered. "Poor Lydia." Her heart went out to the woman. How horrible to think that just this morning they had eaten brunch together and discussed her husband. Now he was gone. She wondered if Lydia had been the one to find his body, then had to push the thought out of her mind because it made her eyes prick with tears. This had been one of the best days of her life, but for Lydia, it had become one of the worst. How could the world be so unfair?

CHAPTER FOUR

T he next day, after a few hours of shopping and waiting around at the hardware store for her paint to finish mixing, Lilah arrived at the sandwich shop ready for a long day of painting and, between coats, baking. She couldn't wait to see what the little shop looked like once the walls were painted the colors she had chosen. After a lot of research and comparing nearly identical colors, she had decided to go with a light powder blue in the main room. Blue, she had read, was supposed to be a soothing, relaxing color. She hoped that with the walls the color of the sky on a summer day, the small room would seem bigger. Her biggest concern was the space feeling cramped once she put in a small table and chairs, and a display in front of the window.

It took another half an hour of taping and laying out plastic — she wanted to update the flooring
 at some point, but wouldn't be able to afford to do so for some time — before she could begin painting. It was with immense satisfaction that she rolled the very first swathe of coat onto the wall.

She was just painting over the last couple of square feet of boring white when she heard a soft knock from behind her. Reid was standing at the shop's front door, which she had propped open with a box fan that was set on low and was blowing the paint fume-infused air out of the building.

"Oh, hi," she said, getting down off of her step stool. "Come on in. I was just finishing up the first coat."

He stepped over the fan and looked around. "It looks nice," he said. "I like the color."

"Thanks. I think it's turning out pretty well." She grabbed her phone and glanced at the time. It was nearly noon. "Are you on your lunch break?"

"No, I had to leave work early," he said. She noticed for the first time that his eyes looked more tired than usual, and he had none of the powerful energy that she was used to. Suddenly she remembered that John Lopez, the man who had been found dead the day before, had been one of his employees.

"I read about what happened," she said. She set the paint roller down on the tray and leaned against the counter. "I'm sorry. Did you know him well?"

"John? No, not very well. He came out drinking with me and some of the guys once in a while, but mostly kept to himself at work." He sighed and ran a hand through his hair. "This whole week has been a mess."

"I heard about some of it. John found out that he was going to be fired, didn't he?" At his surprised look, she explained, "Val came into the diner with his wife, Lydia, yesterday morning before I picked up the keys to this place. She told me about the argument between you and John."

"It was more of a fight than an argument," Reid said. "I think he would have physically attacked me if some of the other guys hadn't held him back. The whole thing was a mess. I don't like laying people off at the best of times. I fought hard to get the extension for them until after Christmas, but now they are still going to be worrying about it during the holidays thanks to him. Though of course now that he's dead, I can't really hold a grudge against him. I just wish things hadn't ended on such a sour note with him."

"Yeah, I can't imagine. It's just terrible all around. I can't imagine anyone at the machine shop is feeling too good today. Is that why you left early?"

Reid's face darkened. "That's another story. Apparently, the police decided I'm a suspect. They showed up at the machine shop this morning to talk to me. My boss at the corporate headquarters called after they left to ask me not to come back in to work until after I had been cleared of any involvement in John's death. They're sending someone else in to take my place temporarily."

"Wow," Lilah said, giving a low whistle. "So, they think he was murdered? The article I read didn't really have much information."

"They must," he said. "But they wouldn't tell me much. Poor guy. I keep wondering what I could have done differently. I didn't kill him, but I might as well have."

"What do you mean?"

"Well, if I hadn't left that letter from corporate on the desk, then he never would have seen it. We wouldn't have had our argument, he wouldn't have gone home early, and then he wouldn't have been in the wrong place when whoever killed him came by."

"You can't blame yourself," Lilah said. "Trust me, I've been there. It's horrible what happened to John, but it's not your fault."

"Thanks for saying that." He gave her a faint smile. "Hey, do you need any help? I'm pretty handy with a paintbrush, and I need something to do now that I'm taking an unexpected vacation from work."

"Sure. Do you want to finish up in here? I'll get started on a batch of cookies. We can eat them while this coat of paint dries."

"That sounds like a plan," he said, picking up the paint roller. "Thanks, Lilah. I needed something to take my mind off of everything."

While Reid finished the first coat of blue paint in the front room, Lilah pulled all of her ingredients out of the grocery bags and lined them up on the counter. She was trying something new today; double chocolate peppermint cookies. She had come across the recipe the night before, and with just a couple of small tweaks, they would be the perfect holiday cookies to make for the shop's grand opening.

She had brought her favorite mixing bowl and cookie sheet from home; her order of new supplies for the cookie shop should be there on Monday. It felt odd to be cooking in such a big kitchen — it wasn't very large compared to the kitchens that larger restaurants had, but compared to her cramped little kitchen, it was huge. She had enough space to spread out all of her ingredients on the counter, and still have room for the printed-out recipe and a bottle of water.

Within just a few minutes, and after just one unfortunate mishap involving the cocoa powder — thankfully she had left the broom in the supply cupboard instead of bringing it home the day before — she had finished mixing all of the ingredients into the chocolate dough. She opened the little glass container of peppermint extract and carefully added a few drops of it to the dough before folding half a bag of the red and green semi-sweet chocolate chips in. She couldn't wait to see how these cookies turned out; if they were good, she would make sure to bring a few to Margie on her way home.

She was just sliding the first batch into the oven when Reid walked into the kitchen. He looked a bit brighter, and there was a smudge of paint on his cheek.

"You really cleaned this place up," he said. "How does everything work?"

"It all seems to work perfectly," she said. "Thank you so much for taking me to see this place when it first came on the market. I really owe you."

"You do, huh?" he said, the corner of his mouth rising in a half grin. "Does that mean I'm finally going to get that date I've been asking you for?"

"Oh, um…" Lilah thought fast. He had asked her out before, but she had always said no. She didn't want to get involved with a man who lived and breathed business. She remembered enough about her own childhood and her parents' marriage to know what it was like to have a husband who was gone all the time. She was too old to waste time on casual dating with someone she wasn't serious about, and she didn't want to risk getting serious about someone who would never be there. On the other hand, Reid *had* been the one to show her this perfect little shop, and he had just had a terrible couple of days. One date surely couldn't hurt… could it?

"Okay," she said at last. "Sure. One date. As a thank you for finding this place for me."

She saw the surprise in his eyes, then his grin turned into a smile. "Can I pick you up at seven on Sunday evening?"

"All right," she said. "That works." She turned her attention back to the oven and spent a few moments searching for the oven light in an attempt to hide how flustered she was. What had she just gotten herself into?

CHAPTER FIVE

"**I**t's just a date."

"A date with *Reid*," Val said. She was grinning ear to ear. "We've been waiting forever for this."

Lilah looked over at Margie, who was also smiling broadly. She knew that the older woman had been trying to set her up with Reid for months. She hadn't been aware that Val had been in on it too.

"Don't get too excited," she said. "It's just one date. I only agreed because I felt bad for him."

"Well don't tell *him* that," Val said. "Men don't like it when you pity them. Just go and have fun. I bet you'll end up enjoying yourself."

"I'm sure it will be a good time," Lilah said. "Reid's a nice guy. But I really shouldn't get involved with anybody right now. I've way too much on my plate to even think about adding a boyfriend to the mess right now."

"Reid will understand about you being busy," Margie chimed in. "He knows what it's like to have to put in long hours. He won't complain."

It was Sunday afternoon, and the three of them were at Lilah's house. Her two friends were helping her get ready for her date, which they seemed to be more excited about than she was. Val was digging through Lilah's closet, trying to find something suitable for a first date, and Margie was sitting on the chair in the corner, watching them and making suggestions. There was already a small pile of discarded dresses on the bed. Lilah didn't see what was wrong with them, but she trusted her friend's judgment. Val was the one with a fiancé, after all, whereas Lilah seemed to be perpetually single.

"Let's see how the date goes before the two of you start trying to marry me off," she said. "Come on, Val, I don't have that many more dresses. There's got to be *something* in my closet that you like."

"You're the one making this difficult," her friend said. "I told you, you should just wear something short and black."

"We're going out to dinner, not getting cocktails at a club," Lilah said, exasperated. "Look, how about this blue dress? It's sort of dressy, and I know it fits me well. I wore it not too long ago. It's a good color, and it doesn't wrinkle easily."

"What do you think?" Val asked, holding it up to show Margie.

"I like it," the older woman said. "That's the one, Lilah. I'm sure it will look very striking on you."

"Right, well, now that we've got that settled, let's go into the kitchen. The two of you are making me anxious about this date. I need something sugary to calm my nerves."

"But we haven't picked out your shoes yet," Val said.

"I only have one pair of shoes that are nice enough to wear with that dress, so that part's easy," Lilah said. "Are you two coming with me or not? I want to eat some cookies before I get into that thing and start on my makeup and hair."

Margie had brought over a platter of cookies, and it was this that Lilah made a beeline towards. She still had a few double chocolate peppermint cookies in her cookie jar, but nothing beat Margie's fresh out of the oven buckeye cookies. She grabbed one and bit into it, closing her eyes as the perfect bite of peanut butter and chocolate seemed to melt in her mouth. Even though her friends were freaking her out a little bit with their excitement, she was happy that they had come over to help her get ready. She didn't regret agreeing to go on the date with Reid, not exactly, but she still wasn't sure she had made the right choice in agreeing to it. What if he asked her out on another date after this, and she said no? Would it make things awkward between them? She hoped not. She didn't want to wreck their friendship.

"So, how is the cookie shop coming?" Margie asked. "I want to try to get out there to see it tomorrow."

"It's really coming along," Lilah said. She nudged the platter of cookies towards Val, who took one. "I finished touching up the paint and taking off all of the tape and plastic this morning. I'm really happy with the color I chose. Oh, and the man I ordered that custom window from said that it should be done by Tuesday. Reid offered to put it in for me if he's still suspended from work by then."

The pane glass window on the cookie shop's front door currently bore the word's *Talbot's Sandwiches*. She was excited to replace it with a new window with her store name. That would be the final touch; after she got the window installed, all that remained would be to set up a display for the front room along with a few more small touches and get the inspection done. Then the store would finally be

48

ready to open. She was trying not to think too hard about the grand opening day. Whenever she did, she began to get hot flashes and a rush of anxiety. What if no one showed up? What if no one wanted to buy cookies? What if the entire thing turned out to be a bust?

"Are you okay?" Val asked. "You look a little bit pale."

"I'm fine," Lilah said. She took another bite out of her cookie and told herself to snap out of it. Her impending date with Reid wasn't helping matters. She didn't understand why she was so nervous about going on a date with someone that she wasn't even interested in romantically.

"Are you worried about your date, dear?" Margie asked. "I'm sorry if Val and I are overwhelming you."

"No, it's not that." She smiled at her friend. "I'm glad the two of you are here. I was just thinking about the cookie shop. I really hope it works out."

"I'm sure it will." Margie patted her hand. "If anyone can make a living selling cookies, it's you."

Lilah thought that her friend's confidence in her might be a bit misplaced, but she was grateful for it anyway.

"Make sure you ask Reid how the police investigation is going," Val said. "He probably knows more than anyone else."

"I doubt they're telling him much, since he's a suspect," Lilah said.

"That's true." Her friend frowned. "You don't think there's any chance he had anything to do with John's death, do you?"

"Of course not." Lilah looked at the other woman in shock. "You know him, too. How could you even think that?"

"I don't think that he would have killed the guy on purpose, but it could have been an accident," Val said. "What if he showed up to talk to John after work, and they got into another fight. A shove at the wrong time could have made John fall into the pool. Maybe he hit his head on the way down, and Reid just panicked."

"If something like that happened, I'm sure Reid would do the right thing and come forward," Margie said.

"I'm just saying it seems like a kind of big coincidence, that's all," Val said with a shrug. "The guy died just hours after he got into a huge argument with Reid. I'm not saying he did it, but I can see why the police are suspicious."

"Now I just feel even worse for him," Lilah said. "If *you* think he might have been involved somehow, then imagine what people who don't even know him must think? I hope all of this gets cleared up quickly. Reid doesn't deserve to be in the spotlight for something like this, not when he already feels terrible as it is for arguing with John before his death."

She finished her cookie and stood up to go get changed. She knew that Val was just tossing her thoughts out there, but still the conversation had unsettled her. Reid hadn't killed anyone, even on accident... had he?

CHAPTER SIX

L ilah opened the door with butterflies in her stomach. She didn't know why she was feeling so nervous — it was just one date, and Reid was a friend. It shouldn't be this big of a deal. Maybe she had eaten something that didn't agree with her, and she was mistaking indigestion for nerves. That was probably it.

"Hi," she said, giving Reid a faint smile. He was a couple of minutes early, but thanks to Val and Margie's help, she was already ready to go. The two women had left a little bit ago. Both were over at Margie's house now, and she was sure that they would pop over to grill her about the date afterward.

"Hi to you." He returned her smile with one of his own. "You look nice."

"Thanks. So do you."

She invited him in while she grabbed her jacket and purse. Her cheeks felt hot. Was she getting a fever? That must be it. Why did things feel so awkward between them right now? She hoped that things would go more smoothly once they were at the restaurant. They just needed a few safe topics to talk about, that was all.

Reid's car was sleek and black, and still smelled new on the inside. She had only been in it a couple of times before, and was always struck by the difference between it and her old blue beater. She liked her car, but she would have traded it in a heartbeat for one as nice as his. Where her engine coughed, his purred.

Sitting on the smooth leather seat and looking out through the tinted window, she was glad that she had listened to Val's advice and had dressed up. If she had worn something more casual, she would have felt out of place next to Reid, who looked very handsome in his black dress shirt and slacks.

"So, where are we off to?" she asked once they had pulled out of her driveway and turned onto the main road.

"There's a place not too far from here that I like," he said. "It's called the Vintage Grill. Have you been there?"

She nodded. "With my parents, a couple of weeks ago. I enjoyed the food."

"But not the parents?" he asked, raising an eyebrow.

"Things have been somewhat strained between myself and my father ever since I left my job at his company," she told him. "Me telling him about the cookie shop didn't exactly help matters."

"Ah," he said. "I'm sorry. I'm sure he'll come around eventually."

"I hope so. I sent him an invitation to the grand opening, but he hasn't responded yet."

"Well, you can count on me to be there," he said. "And Val and Margie too, I'm sure."

"I know." She smiled at him. "Thanks."

Reid had made reservations at the Vintage Grill, so they were seated almost immediately. Lilah hadn't eaten much besides the cookies that Margie brought over earlier that evening, and her stomach began to growl at the succulent scents coming from the kitchen.

"Here are our holiday menus," the host said as he seated them. "Someone will be with you shortly to take your drink orders. Our wines are listed on the back."

She and Reid chose a white wine together, then read through their menus in silence for a couple of moments. Lilah was happy to focus on choosing her meal; it delayed the moment when she would have to figure out what to talk about with Reid. She had never been good at first dates. Or second dates, come to think of it.

"I don't know what to get," she said. "Everything looks so good."

"I think the holiday menu is only around for about three weeks," he told her. "They switch it out right after Christmas. I've tried a few of the choices over the years. I think the quail was the best, but none of them will disappoint you."

"I'll go with the quail then," she said. Glazed quail with house pomegranate sauce, mashed cauliflower, and roasted mushrooms and vegetables sounded good to her, and she didn't think she had ever tried quail before. Even if the rest of the date turned out to be awkward, at least she would end up with a delicious meal.

"Do you need any more help at the cookie shop?" Reid asked her once they had placed their orders. "Other than installing the new window."

"I don't think so," Lilah told him. "I might need some help moving the table and chairs for the front room in, and I still haven't found a good display rack, but other than that, pretty much all that needs to be done is the inspection. If everything goes well, I should be able to open before Christmas like I wanted to."

"That's wonderful," he said. "I'm glad. I can't wait to see how the cookie shop does."

Their conversation proceeded smoothly after that. It wasn't anywhere near as awkward as she had dreaded. In fact, it was hard for her to admit, even to herself, but she liked Reid. He was nice, intelligent, and good looking. He always tried to help her out. And not just her, but all of his friends. She remembered everything that he had done for Margie over the years, from fixing a rotted board on the porch to repairing a leak in the roof. He had never accepted any pay besides the containers of baked goods the older woman pressed on him. From what she had seen of him with his niece and nephew at the corn maze a few months ago, he was good with kids, too.

Maybe dating him wouldn't be as bad as I thought, she thought. *He does always make time for his family and friends. Just because he spends a lot of time at his job doesn't mean he's too busy to have a normal life.*

She shook her head, trying to clear it of dangerous thoughts. She was just letting herself get wooed by a nice meal and some good conversation. She didn't need the distraction that a serious boyfriend would bring, not while she was trying to build a business.

Then, of course, she had to consider what Val had said earlier. Was it possible that Reid was somehow involved in John's death? Looking at him as he laughed at a joke she had made, she found it hard to even consider the possibility. She had never seen anything to suggest that he wasn't a good man. And yet, she couldn't deny that it was a big coincidence that John had died just hours after a major, embarrassing argument with his boss.

* * *

"Thank you," she said when he dropped her off at her house a couple of hours later. "I had a really nice time."

"Me too," he said. "Oh, there's something I've been meaning to ask you all night."

She tensed. Was he going to ask her on a second date? What would she say?

"I think I left a jacket at the cookie shop when I stopped by to help paint the other day. Would you mind looking for it next time you're there? No hurry, but if it isn't there, then I'll have to try to figure out where else I could have left it."

"Oh. Of course," she said, trying not to feel too disappointed. "I'll look for it tomorrow."

"Thanks." He smiled. "I should get going now. I think Val and Margie might murder me if I make them wait any longer to come over here."

They both glanced over to Margie's house, where the silhouettes of the two women could be seen watching them eagerly from the window. Lilah laughed. She might have been embarrassed if he was a stranger, but Reid knew them both well enough to require no explanation.

"Good night, Lilah," he said.

"Good night, Reid."

For a moment, she thought he was going to kiss her, but then he just smiled and walked away. She gazed after him, feeling confused to her core, until he drove around the corner and out of sight.

CHAPTER SEVEN

L ilah worked the morning shift at the diner the next day. Waking up at six thirty to go to work wasn't fun, especially when she had stayed up nearly to midnight the night before. Still, she felt pretty good once she had a couple of cups of coffee in her. She made sure to down another cup before leaving the diner at noon, and hoped that the jitters from the caffeine would fade by the time she got to the cookie shop. Having double the responsibility was already starting to take its toll on her, and the cookie shop wasn't even open yet.

She met up with Val at her house before heading to the shop. Her friend had volunteered to help her touch up the trim in the kitchen and do a few other small tasks. In return, Lilah was going to treat them to lunch at the little deli on the corner. The soups and sandwiches they served were much healthier than what they offered at the diner, and Lilah could only eat so much fried food before she started to crave something more wholesome.

"It's a nice day," her friend said as they drove along the main road into town. "You know, that's one of the things I like best about Alabama. I lived in Michigan for a year after college, and the winters there are ten times worse than this. You'd never get away with just wearing a light jacket in mid-December up there."

"Yeah, it's hard to complain about the climate down here," Lilah said. "I forget how lucky we are sometimes. Both of us are doing pretty well, aren't we? I mean, we aren't rich by any means, but we're happy and we're doing what we want to be doing."

"That's what counts," her friend said. "I've never understood why some people focus so much on making money that they forget to be happy. What's the point of all of that if you're miserable at the end of the day?"

"I don't know." Lilah looked over at her old college roommate and smiled. "Thanks. You're making me feel better. Just this morning I was worrying about what I was going to do if the cookie shop doesn't bring in as much money as I hoped. It's important that I don't forget why I'm doing all of this; because I enjoy it."

"That's the spirit. I don't think you have anything to worry about, though," Val said.

CRUNCHY CHRISTMAS MURDER BOOK FOUR IN KILLER COOKIE COZY MYSTERIES

True to her word, the first thing Lilah did when they got to the cookie shop was to look for Reid's jacket. Since she didn't remember seeing it over the weekend, she didn't expect to find it, so was surprised when Val discovered it behind the counter in the front room.

"It must have fallen to the floor at some point," she said. "He's lucky it didn't get any paint on it."

"I'll call him and let him know," Lilah said.

She set the jacket on the counter in the kitchen next to her purse and dialed Reid's number.

"Great, I'm glad it's there," he said when she told him about the jacket. "I can come and pick it up now if you'd like."

Val, who had followed her into the kitchen, mouthed something. Lilah covered the phone with her hand.

"What?" she whispered.

"Tell him we'll drop it off. There's a new coffee shop not far from his house that I've been meaning to check out. We might as well kill two birds with one stone."

"Val and I can drop it off," Lilah said to Reid. "It'll be about an hour; I want to finish touching up the trim at the cookie shop first so it can dry while we're out. I'll text you when we're on our way."

She had never been to Reid's house before, but Val knew the way. He lived in a nice neighborhood a few miles outside of town. The houses had large yards and were spread out. She slowed down as she followed her friend's increasingly unsure directions, feeling very conscious of how loud her little car was.

"It's that one," Val said at last. Seeing her friend's look, she added, "I'm sure… I think."

"I thought you'd been here before," Lilah said.

"Only once. He needed someone to stop in and feed his fish while he was gone for the weekend, and I guess his sister was out of town. It was a year ago, my memory isn't *that* good. I know he lives near Lydia, that's how I got us this far."

"Lydia?" Lilah asked. "As in Lydia Lopez, the woman whose husband died?"

"That's the one," Val said.

"I didn't realize they lived near Reid."

Lilah frowned as they climbed out of the car, her mind racing. She hadn't put much weight on Val's suspicions before, but she hadn't realized how close Reid lived to the man who had died. No wonder the police viewed him as a major suspect. He lived within walking distance of the murder victim.

Val knocked on the door and gave Lilah an *I-told-you-so* glance when Reid answered. He met Lilah's eyes and a concerned crease appeared between his eyebrows.

"Is everything okay?" he asked. "You look worried."

"Yeah, I'm fine," she said, giving herself a shake and forcing a smile. "Here's your jacket. It fell behind the counter somehow."

"Thanks," he said. "And thanks for driving it all the way out here."

"No problem," she assured him. "It's a nice day for a drive, and it was good to clear the paint fumes out of our systems."

"Do you two want to come in?" he asked. "I don't have much to offer, unfortunately. Some beer… I could make coffee."

"Thanks for the offer," Val said. "But we were going to stop at Cafe Latte to try out their new drinks. Do you want to come with?"

"I do, but I can't," he said reluctantly. "I have a call with my lawyer scheduled in half an hour. He's trying to figure out this mess. I'm going stir crazy without anything to do. I never thought I'd want to get back to work this badly."

"We'll see you later, then," Lilah said. "I hope your call goes well."

"Thanks. I'll call you tonight."

Val was smirking when they got back into the little blue car.

"What?" Lilah asked.

"Oh, just the two of you. I love watching romances develop."

"It's not…" She sighed, realizing arguing with her friend would be a losing battle; in part, because she wasn't even too sure that Val was wrong. "Come on, let's just go get that coffee."

Val took them a different way out of the neighborhood than how they came in. Lilah slowed down as they approached a house that had what looked like dozens of flower bouquets on the porch.

"That's where Lydia lives," her friend said. "People keep bringing her flowers and food. She brought them in at first, but I think it's just getting to be too much for her. They mean well, but a bunch of dead roses aren't going to help her deal with John's death."

"That's sad," Lilah said, letting the engine idle. "It's hard to imagine what she's going through."

A knock on her window startled her. She turned her head to see a balding man wearing a reindeer sweater peering in at her. She rolled down the window, and he poked his head in.

"I just wanted to make sure you found the right house," he said. "That's me." He jerked his thumb over his shoulder towards a house that was decked out in Christmas cheer, complete with an animatronic Santa Claus in the yard. "I can help you carry the two liters up."

"I'm sorry," Lilah said. "I have absolutely no idea what you're talking about."

"Oh, my gosh, you aren't the pizza delivery person?" He looked into the back seat of her car as if expecting to see a pizza box. "Sorry, miss. My mistake."

"I'm sure they'll be here soon," she said, beginning to roll up the window. The man stuck his arm in, blocking her.

"Chris," he said. "Chris Burk."

"Nice to meet you." She shook his hand quickly, feeling completely befuddled by the situation. What was with this guy? "Have a nice day."

"Merry Christmas!" he called as she pulled away. "And a happy New Year!"

CHAPTER EIGHT

"Thanks for helping out," Margie said. "I know you must be busy."

"There actually isn't much left to do at the shop," Lilah said. "Reid helped me install the window yesterday, and I found the perfect table and chair set, and a nice little display rack to go in the front window. All that's really left to do is the inspection, which is happening tomorrow. It's nice to take a little break before the grand opening. Besides, I always enjoy learning new recipes with you."

She had finally set a date for the grand opening; the Thursday before Christmas. She and Val had hung a banner in the front window to announce it, and she had made sure that everyone close to her could attend. Even her father was planning on coming, which she felt was a big step for the two of them.

"I'll be sure to tell everyone that you helped," Margie said. "This charity raffle means a lot to a lot of people in the area; I know they'll be grateful."

The older woman was constantly involved with charities and volunteering to help at local events. Today, the two of them were going to be baking a couple dozen cookies for a charity auction. The winner would get a basket of cookies, and a gift card to Lilah's new shop. It was good advertising for the cookie shop, and, of course, a nice thing to do for the holidays.

The first cookies on their list were basic chocolate chip cookies. They were a popular recipe for a reason, and never got old. Lilah was sure she could make them with her eyes closed. As she reached for a bag of semi-sweet chocolate chips, she had an idea.

"Hey, since this is a holiday charity event, what do you think about spicing it up a little?" she said. "I've got some festive red and green chocolate chips at my house. I can run over and get them if you want."

"That's a great idea," Margie said. "I'll get the dough ready while you go get them."

Lilah hurried over to her house, glad that she lived so close. It was wonderful to have one of her best friends as a neighbor. She didn't know what she would do when she moved one day.

She was digging through her cupboard for the chocolate chips, keeping Winnie back absentmindedly with her leg, when her phone rang. She pulled it out of her pocket, and wasn't surprised to see it was Reid. He had been calling her every day since their date. She didn't mind. In fact, she enjoyed their conversations. He always seemed interested to hear about the cookie shop, and gave her encouragement when she needed it. She just wished things were going as well for him; he was still on unpaid leave from his job, and neither of them knew if the police were making any progress on the murder case.

She hadn't thought as much about John's murder as she would have if she hadn't been distracted by the looming opening of the cookie shop. When she did take the time to mull it over, she found it chilling that no one seemed to have any idea what had happened. All the public knew was that he had been found dead in his pool. His wife might know more, but she wasn't about to go and bother the poor woman for answers. All she could do was hope that the killer would be found soon. Reid deserved to have his name cleared, and Lydia deserved peace.

Lilah bit her lip as she stared at her cell phone. She felt bad ignoring the call, but she was supposed to be helping Margie right now. Plus, Reid had been hinting about them going on another date, and she wasn't sure what she would say if he asked her. She had enjoyed their last date, and there had definitely been a spark there, but she still had most of the same reservations about a relationship with him that she had before. Besides, she was going to be so busy with the grand opening that she didn't know when she would have time to go out.

The ringing stopped. She had waited too long to make up her mind, and it had gone to voicemail. Lilah mentally promised Reid that she would call him back later, then shoved the phone in her pocket and continued her search for the festive chocolate chips.

When she got back to Margie's, the older woman had the small television in her kitchen on and was watching the news. She waved Lilah over as soon as she came in.

"Look at this," she said. "It's about Reid."

Lilah put down the bag of semi-sweet chocolate chips and listened the news anchor.

"A suspect in a local murder case was arrested this morning, and has just been released on bail. The man refused to comment." The video footage showed Reid walking out of the local courthouse with a small, thin man next to him whom Lilah assumed was his lawyer.

The footage switched to something else, and she turned to Margie with a guilty look on her face. "Oh my goodness, that must be what he just called me about," she said. "I let it go to voicemail since I was busy. I feel terrible now."

"Go call him back," Margie said. "The cookies can wait."

Lilah hurried into the other room and redialed Reid's number. It went to voicemail, and she left him a quick message telling him what she had seen. A moment later, she got a text from him.

With my lawyer now. I'll call you later.

She had no choice but to put the phone back in her pocket and go finish baking the cookies with her friend while she waited. Her mind raced as she wondered what in the world was happening. Why had Reid gotten arrested? Had the police found some evidence against him? If so, did that mean that Reid was the killer?

CHAPTER NINE

R eid called her back later that evening. She answered his call immediately, anxious to hear what had happened.

"I'm fine," he told her. "My lawyer thinks he can get the police to drop the charges. Things should turn out okay."

"What happened, though?" she asked. "Why did they bring you in in the first place?"

"All I know is they got an eyewitness statement from a neighbor that they saw someone matching my description go into John's yard around the time of death. Thankfully we have cameras at the machine shop, and once the judge reviews the footage, he'll see that I couldn't possibly have been there at the time the neighbor said I was."

Lilah felt a rush of relief. Not only would the charges against Reid get dropped, but video evidence that he was at work during the time that the murder happened, had to be pretty solid. Hopefully he would be completely removed from the case as a suspect. She couldn't believe that she had doubted him earlier. She shouldn't have let herself believe that he would kill someone, accidentally or not, even for a second.

"It's good that you have proof that you were at work when all of this happened," she said. "Do you think the neighbor was lying, or does the killer just look a lot like you?"

"I don't know," Reid said. "To be honest, I don't even know if they're sure that John was murdered."

"What do you mean?" Lilah asked, surprised.

"Well, I talked to Lydia after I got home, and she said that John had been found in the pool with a head injury. Now, I don't like to say this about a dead man, but everyone knew that he had a bit of an alcohol problem. It wouldn't surprise me at all if he started drinking when he got home after that scene at work. I don't know why he would have gone out to the pool in this weather, but, well, you see where I'm going."

"You think he got drunk and fell into the pool?" Lilah asked. "He just hit his head… and drowned?"

"That's what his wife thinks happened," he told her. "She thinks that the only reason the police are so reluctant to declare his death an accident is because of how large his life insurance policy was. I'm sure my argument with him right before he died isn't helping matters either."

Lilah's eyes went wide. She remembered Lydia saying something about her husband's life insurance policy shortly before he died. She had even joked about using the life insurance money to support herself after he got laid off. At least, she was pretty sure that it had been a joke… but what if it hadn't?

"Lilah?"

Reid's voice brought her back to their conversation.

"Sorry," she said. "I was just lost in thought. I'm glad you didn't have to wait at the jail long. I'm sorry I didn't answer earlier — I was helping Margie bake some cookies."

"Don't worry about it," he said. "I just wanted to make sure you heard what had happened from me first. I don't know what they're going to say about all of this in the newspapers."

"If there's video of you at the machine shop while the murder was taking place, no one will seriously believe that you did it," she said. "I don't think you have anything to worry about."

"That's good to hear," he said. "Thank you. So, how was your day?"

Lilah switched him to speaker phone as they spoke so that she could text Val. She had a sneaking suspicion that Lydia knew more than she was letting on about her husband's death, and she was determined to get to the bottom of it.

Val met her as planned at the diner the next day an hour before her shift was supposed to start. Lilah handed her an eggnog shake, and the two of them sat at the counter to discuss their plan. The diner was empty, other than Kate and Randall in the kitchen, so they didn't bother keeping their voices down.

"How well do you know Lydia?" Lilah asked her friend.

"We've been friends for a couple of years," Val said. "We aren't super close, but we get together every once in a while, for shopping or lunch. Before she worked for the florist, she worked at my favorite antique shop, which is how we met."

"Do you think I'm crazy to suspect her?"

Val hesitated. "Well, not exactly. I can't say the thought didn't cross my mind. She did fight with her husband a lot, but at the end of the day I always thought they loved each other. But in these sorts of cases, the police *always* look at the spouse as a possible suspect. Especially when life insurance is involved. I don't think they'd miss it if she was the one that killed him."

"It's not like the police are always right," Lilah pointed out. "I mean, they arrested Reid, and that was obviously wrong."

Her friend shrugged. "I really don't know. I can't imagine Reid *or* Lydia would have killed him on purpose. But either of them could have gotten into a fight with him and done it on accident. I bet John was in a pretty bad mood after having the police called on him at work."

"What do you think of Reid's theory?" Lilah asked her.

"That he got drunk and fell into the pool on his own?" Val shrugged. "It's possible. I'm just as curious as you are about what happened, but there are just too many ways he could have died. I hate to say it, but John was one of those people that was just really good at making people mad. He had his good traits, too, but from what Lydia has said, he's annoyed enough people over the years to have quite the list of enemies."

Lilah ate the cherry off the top of her shake as she mulled over their conversation. Other than feeling bad for his wife, she hadn't been paying much attention to John's death. Now that Reid had gotten arrested, however, some sort of protective feeling seemed to have risen inside her. She just wanted the case solved and Reid's name to be cleared. Was that too much to ask?

CHAPTER TEN

A call from her mother the next morning put all thought of John's murder out of her mind.

"You want to stay here?" Lilah said, certain that she had heard wrong. "Until Wednesday?"

"Yes, dear. I'm sure you could use the help. With your new business opening in just a few days, I can't even imagine how busy you must be. You're my daughter, and this is a big step for you. I want to help."

Lilah closed her eyes and took a deep breath. She loved her mother, but they were lucky if they could go a few hours without finding something to argue about. She knew the woman meant well by offering to stay with her for the next few days and help her get ready for the grand opening, but she wasn't sure that her mother's presence would help with the stress at all. In fact, it might have the opposite effect. Still, she couldn't imagine saying no to the offer, not right before the holidays, and not when she finally seemed to be coming around and supporting Lilah's goal of opening the cookie shop.

"Great," Lilah said in a falsely cheery voice that any other woman would have seen right through. "When can I expect you?"

"I thought I'd leave here around noon. I should be to your house by three. Does that work for you?"

"Yep, I'll see you then."

She hung up the phone, trying not to panic as she looked around the kitchen. She needed to clean. She needed to clean *everything* and finish the laundry, and figure out something to make for dinner that didn't come pre-cooked and frozen.

"Calm down," she muttered to herself. "It's just Mom."

Whenever her parents visited, she had the same reaction. She couldn't help the feeling wanting to prove herself to them. She knew that a lot of her choices had disappointed them, and she wanted to show them that she did know what she was doing, after all. She was anxious to have everything perfect for her mother's arrival — but that would have to wait. She glanced at the time on her phone. In twenty minutes, she was supposed to meet the guy at the cookie shop for the inspection. After that, she would come back and clean up.

"Everything looks good."

"Really? Thank you so much. You have no idea how nervous I was."

The health inspector smiled. "I used to inspect this kitchen every year, when that sandwich guy owned it. I know he bought quality equipment and kept everything up to code, so he won half the battle for you. What happened to him, anyway? He retire?"

"He passed away," Lilah told him.

"Oh. I'm sorry to hear that." He fell silent for a moment, then shook himself. "He was a good guy, and cared a lot about this place. It seems like you're taking good care of it. I'm sure he would approve. Come on, follow me back to the truck and I'll sign the commercial kitchen certification license for you."

She watched as he scribbled on a pad of paper, ripped off the top piece, and handed it to her. "There you go. You keep this. It has to be displayed prominently in your kitchen. A lot of people frame theirs. The other copy goes with me back to the health department. I'll see you next year."

He gave her a little wave, then climbed into his truck. She watched as he drove away, then looked down at the piece of paper in her hands. This was the last thing she had needed to achieve before being able to open the store, and she had done it. It was hard to believe.

Grinning, she went back inside and set the certification on the counter. She would pick up a frame for it later today. This was it. She was really going to be able to open the cookie shop on Wednesday. Suddenly even the prospect of her mother staying with her for a few days didn't seem bad.

Her good mood remained the entire time that she cleaned her house. She even gave Winnie a bath, and clipped Oscar's nails. Everything would be just perfect for her mother's visit. She felt like the weight of the world had been lifted off of her shoulders now that she had passed the inspection. She hadn't realized just how worried about it she had been until after the fact.

Her mother knocked on the door shortly after three, and gave Lilah a big hug when she opened the door.

"I read your text. Congratulations, sweetie," she said.

"Thanks, Mom. Come on in. I'm making chicken soup for dinner; it's in the crock pot now. We've got a few hours until it's time to eat, and I'm free for the rest of the day. What do you want to do?"

"I want to see the cookie shop, of course," her mother said. "What name did you decide on."

"You'll have to wait and see," Lilah said with a smile.

The two of them stood in front of the cookie shop. Lilah looked at it with a critical eye, trying to see it as her mother did. She had grown so used to it that it was hard to look at it with fresh eyes.

"The Casual Cookie. I like it."

"You do?" Lilah asked. "Settling on a name was probably one of the hardest things I've done."

"It's catchy and easy to remember," her mother said. "That's always good for a business name. You don't want to have something that no one can pronounce. I think it's a great choice. Now, do I get to see inside?"

"Of course, let's go in."

She unlocked the door and held it open for the older woman, hitting the light switch on the wall as she followed her.

"This is how it will look on opening day," she said. "Except there will be cookies in the display cases, and hopefully a lot more people."

"It's wonderful, darling. You obviously have a gift for this sort of thing. I'm sorry I didn't see it earlier."

"It's all right," Lilah told her. "I had my share of doubts too, don't worry. But I think this will turn out okay."

"Oh, it's going to be fantastic. I can't wait for your father to see this. He'll be so proud."

"I'd settle for him not being angry," Lilah said with a dry laugh. "The kitchen's back here. I'll show you around. I think you'll like how much counter space there is."

CHAPTER ELEVEN

Having her mother stay with her wasn't as bad as Lilah had thought it would be. In fact, it was kind of nice to have time for just the two of them to bond. With the cookie shop ready to open, all she had to do was her normal shifts at the diner, and some last-minute grocery shopping for the big day. She planned on making all of the cookies for the grand opening fresh the morning of, so there wasn't much she could do in the way of preparation.

The day before the cookie shop's grand opening Lilah's nerves began to get the better of her again. She had the morning shift at the diner, so when she clocked out, she found herself with an entire afternoon of free time looming in front of her. She normally would have enjoyed it, especially since it would probably be her last afternoon completely free for a long time, but was too nervous about tomorrow to do anything other than pace and constantly reread her homemade book of recipes.

"Lilah, what are you doing?" her mother asked as she walked through the living room for the third time.

"I don't know," she admitted. "I forgot what I came in here for."

"Let's get out of the house," the older woman suggested. "I know, let's go get you a Christmas tree."

With everything that had been going on, Lilah hadn't had time to put up her fake tree. It was still buried in a box in one of the closets somewhere. She hadn't had a real tree for years, not because she didn't like them, but because it seemed like such a hassle to go out to the tree farm and get one, and then figure out how to dispose of it a few weeks later.

"I don't know," she said. "I wasn't going to put one up this year. I've been so busy, and things are only going to get busier after the Casual Cookie opens. I probably won't remember to take it down until June, and by then it will be a dried-out husk of a fire hazard."

"I'll call you next month and remind you to get rid of it," her mother said. "Let's go. It will be fun. Just like when you were younger. You used to love getting trees, remember?"

She knew when she was beat. The two of them had been getting along so well; it would be nice to do one last family activity before the big day. Besides, she did love walking into the living room to see a brightly lit tree on Christmas morning. It was just the putting it up and taking it down that she didn't enjoy so much.

"All right, all right. Let's take your car, though. I don't know if mine could handle carrying a Christmas tree."

There was only one small tree farm near Vista. The sign out front said *Brown Family Tree Farm*. It was a small affair, and the pickings were slim this close to the holiday. Still, Lilah had to admit that it was fun to walk through the muddy farm with her mother, trying to find a tree that looked like it might fit in her house.

"How about this one?" her mother suggested.

"It's got a bald spot on this side," Lilah said as she walked around to the other side.

"Well, you could just put that side towards the wall."

"I suppose." She frowned at it. "I guess it's the best one here. I'll go find someone to help us."

She wandered back up the road towards the front of the tree farm where there was a small wooden building for the farm's employees. She raised a hand to knock on the door, and was surprised when it opened before she even touched it. The man who came out was one that she recognized, though it took her a moment to place him, possibly due to his Santa Clause costume.

"Hi," he said brightly. "Have you made your tree selection?"

"I think so. Hey, didn't I meet you a few days ago?" she said. "You thought I was the pizza delivery driver."

He squinted at her. "Oh, I did, didn't I? I'm sorry about that. I always wait outside for them, in case they need help carrying anything in. When I saw your car roll up and idle at the curb, I was sure you had the pizzas."

"Sorry for the confusion," she said. "A friend of mine knows one of your neighbors, and she was just showing me where her house was, since we were in the neighborhood."

"The Lopez's?" he asked. "It's a pity what happened to them, isn't it?"

"It is," Lilah agreed. "Did you know John well?"

"Not very well. He wasn't very outgoing. He didn't seem like a very happy man. He never even decorated for Christmas, even though it's something our homeowners' association agreed on — everyone should put at least something up. It used to drive me crazy." He laughed and shook his head. "Well, you saw my house. I'm a big fan of the holidays. I volunteer here every year, and go caroling on Christmas Eve. Christmas is my favorite holiday. Everyone is so cheerful and happy. I don't understand how some people can hate it so much."

"I doubt he hated Christmas," Lilah said. "He probably just didn't feel like putting up decorations just to have to take them down again in a few weeks. I know I sure didn't. My mother dragged me into this. She's waiting by the tree we picked out now, so we don't forget which one it is."

He chuckled. "Then we should probably get going." He ducked back inside the shed and came out with a hand saw. "Lead on."

It wasn't until Lilah was standing next to her mother, watching Chris saw through the tree's trunk that she realized he might have seen something on the day that John was murdered. She kicked herself mentally for not asking him about it when they were talking. Even the smallest clue might be enough to clear Reid's name in time for Christmas.

CHAPTER TWELVE

L ilah woke up at four thirty the next morning, her heart fluttering with excitement in her chest as she stared up at the dark ceiling. Today was the day. At noon, she would open the doors of the Casual Cookie to the public for the first time. A thousand worries and doubts rushed through her mind. Would anyone even show up? What if she got into the kitchen and forgot everything she had learned over the past few months? There were countless things that could go wrong. If anything bad did happen, she knew that she would just have to figure out how to deal with it in the moment. Right now, she needed to get up and get dressed. She had a big day in front of her.

She padded barefoot into the kitchen to start the coffee. A soft glow came from the living room where her mom was sleeping on the pullout couch. She peeked into the room and smiled to see the Christmas tree lit up. The two of them had spent the evening before decorating it, and she knew that those would be hours that she would remember forever.

Trying to be as quiet as possible so as not to wake up her mother, Lilah got dressed and downed the first of what would be many cups of coffee that day. She scribbled a note for her mother and left it on the counter, then slipped out the front door and got into her car. Val, Margie, and her mother would all be meeting her there in a few hours, but she wanted this early morning time to begin baking by herself.

As she walked through the back entrance into the cookie shop's kitchen, she flipped the switch on the wall and the building hummed to life around her. She was unable to control the grin that spread across her face at the sight of the clean, beautiful kitchen that was all hers. Brand new sets of mixing bowls, spoons, and cookies sheets were tucked away into the cupboards, and the fridge, freezer, and pantry were full of ingredients. It had taken her quite a few shopping trips, but it had paid off; the kitchen was stocked with anything and everything she could ever want to make any type of cookie that struck her fancy. The health inspection certificate was framed and hung on the wall beside the freezer, and she took a moment to walk over to it and examine it again. Somehow that little piece of paper felt more official to her than all of the other stuff. She loved the sight of her business name printed on the dotted line. It made everything feel that much more real.

"Time to get started," she said to herself, her voice sounding loud in the empty building. "I've got some cookies to bake."

By the time her friends and her mother arrived, she had two batches of cookies cooked to perfection and cooling on racks on the counter. She had started off simple with chocolate chip cookies and peanut butter cookies, but the next few types that she planned on making would be a bit more complex. She was going to include cookie cups in her lineup, and those always took a bit longer to make. Plus, they would have to frost the sugar cookies and decorate them for the holiday. She was grateful for all of their help, but especially for Margie's. Her neighbor was worth ten normal women when it came to baking, and Lilah would need all of the help that she could get today.

The preparations may have gone more smoothly if Lilah had been more comfortable delegating tasks to her family and friends, but she felt the need to check and double check everything on her own. She wanted things to be perfect today of all days, which meant that she was constantly dashing back and forth from the kitchen to the front room, switching gears between baking and setting up the displays. Val had brought a string of Christmas lights to make the shop look more festive, and by late morning, people were beginning to pause as they passed the front window and peer inside hungrily.

"Lilah, Reid just texted me — he didn't want to interrupt you in case you were busy — and wanted to know if there's anything you need him to bring," Val said when Lilah came back into the kitchen to grab another tray of cookies to bring to the front.

"Um, I don't think so…" she looked around wildly, trying to think of anything they might be lacking. "Water, maybe. Bottled water. I think we're almost out."

"I'll let him know."

Her friend hurried away. Lilah noticed her mother give her a sharp look. The older woman followed her into the front room.

"Who's Reid?" she asked.

"He's a friend," Lilah said, carefully placing red velvet cookies on the display rack.

"Just a friend?"

"We went on a date," she told her mother. "But just one." She looked up to see her mother's smiling face. "What?"

"Oh, I'm just happy. Your father and I worry about you, you know. All alone in this small town… and you're getting older, you know. If you want to have kids, it's going to have to be sooner rather than later."

"Mom, it was one date," Lilah said, biting back a sigh. This was why she never told the woman these sorts of things. If her parents had their way, she would have been married off right out of college, and would have two kids by now. She had tried telling her mother that starting a family in her thirties wasn't exactly unheard of these days, but she never seemed to listen.

"Well, he seems like a nice guy. I hope you have a second date."

"You don't even know him!"

"He offered to buy you water," her mother said over her shoulder as she returned to the kitchen. "That's something."

CHAPTER THIRTEEN

"It's almost time," Lilah said. She felt dizzy. She knew she was on the verge of hyperventilating, but she couldn't help it. This was it. The clock was minutes away from striking noon. What in the world had she been thinking of when she decided to start her own business? How had she been crazy enough to go through with it?

"We'll clear out of here," Val said. "We'll come in the front in a few minutes to make the store look busier. Maybe I'll even be your first customer."

"Don't be silly, you don't have to pay," she told her friend.

"That's a nice sentiment and all, but I don't mine handing over a couple of dollars to help my best friend's store."

"But —"

Val held up a hand. "Don't even try to argue. You buy stuff from me at the boutique all the time."

There wasn't anything she could come up with to refute her friend's logic, so she shrugged. "Fine. You win. You might be my only customer, anyway. At least I'll make one sale today."

"Don't be so hard on yourself," her mother chimed in. "You saw how many people were interested in the store this morning. I'm sure some of them will be back."

"I put up your flyers at the library and in the recreation center at my church," Margie said. "I know quite a few ladies from there are planning on coming. You'll have plenty of customers today."

"Yeah, all you have to do is convince them to come back," Val said with a smile. "But that shouldn't be hard, not after they try the cookies."

Her friends and mother left, giving her a few minutes of peace and quiet in the kitchen before she went out front to unlock the doors and open the store up for her customers for the very first time. She was so overwhelmed that she didn't even know what she was feeling. Excitement, terror, doubt, joy... all the emotions joined together in a mix that made her feel shaky and somewhat sick to her stomach.

"The Casual Cookie," she said to the kitchen. "It's not a dream anymore. This is real." A glance at the clock showed her that it was time to go and open the doors.

***

"Thanks for coming to the Casual Cookie," she said. "Have a nice day."

Her fifth customer, an elderly woman who had paid in quarters, walked away clutching the paper bag with a double chocolate peppermint cookie inside. Lilah looked over the line of people waiting and grinned. She couldn't have been happier with the turnout. The store had only been open for a few minutes, and she had already made five sales. She wondered when she would stop counting.

"Hi, can I have one of those Santa sugar cookies, and a snicker-doodle?" her next customer said. "Thanks."

"Here you go. Thanks for shopping at the Casual Cookie. Have a nice day."

"You, too. Hey, do you do deliveries? My daughter's birthday is next month, and she's never been a fan of cake. I don't know anywhere else in town that makes homemade cookies. Could you do princess themed ones?"

"I can deliver after or before the store's normal hours," Lilah told the woman. "It's just me working here for now, so I can't go anywhere while the store is open. And I can make any type of cookies that you want."

"Perfect." The woman smiled at her. "I'll be back later this week with an order. I've got to see what my daughter wants first."

The next few hours passed in a blur. Val, Margie, and Lilah's mother stopped in twice to see how she was doing and buy another couple of cookies. The Casual Cookie was hardly ever empty; the turnout was so much better than Lilah had expected that she began to wonder if she had made enough cookies for the day. She had made extra dough for the more popular flavors, but finding the time to run back and pop another batch in the oven could be problematic. If things kept going this well, then she would almost need to hire an employee just to keep things running smoothly.

"I'll take a brownie cup cookie, please," a man's voice said. Lilah looked up from the case to see Reid standing there. He had stopped by briefly before the cookie shop had opened to drop off the bottled water, but this was the first time she had seen him since.

"Here you go," she said. "And no, don't pay me. I'm serious. I'm only accepting money from Val because she made me."

"If you insist," he said. "I'll just put it towards our second date." He raised an eyebrow.

Lilah hesitated, then smiled. She liked Reid. It shouldn't matter that he didn't match up perfectly to her ideal idea of what she wanted in a boyfriend. He was a good man, he obviously liked her, and, well, he was definitely good looking enough for the both of them. Maybe it was time to just go with it and see how things ended up. "All right, that sounds like a deal," she said. "I'll hold you to it."

"I'll stop in this evening before close and we can make plans," he promised. "Thanks for the cookie. You're doing wonderfully, Lilah. Keep up the good work."

After Reid left, Lilah barely glanced at the clock again until the sun started to fall in the sky. She had decided to make the weekday hours noon to six, at least until she could quit her diner job and work at the Casual Cookie full time. There was only about an hour left to go this first day. Even though she had enjoyed the numerous sales immensely, she was beginning to get tired. It would feel good to close up and go home. She just hoped that the shop was as successful tomorrow as it had been today.

"Welcome to the Casual Cookie," she said brightly when the front door swung open again. This time she recognized the woman who walked through the doors. "Oh, hi, Lydia. It's nice of you to stop by."

"Thanks." The woman gave her a wan smile. "I needed a reason to get out of the house."

The front door opened again. Lydia looked behind her and visibly paled when she saw who was coming in. "Sorry," she said quickly, turning back to Lilah. "Do you have a bathroom I can use?"

"Right through there."

"Thanks."

Lilah turned her gaze to the man who had just come in; she recognized Officer Eldridge, one of only a small number of Vista police officers. He was staring after Lydia, his brow creased in a frown. Lilah was prepared to guess that he was having the exact same thought that she was; why on earth had Lydia Lopez fled at the sight of him?

CHAPTER FOURTEEN

"**D**o you know her?" he asked in a low voice, leaning towards Lilah from across the counter.

"She's a friend of a friend," she said. "Is there something I can help you with?" She wasn't quite sure whether she was asking about the cookies, or information about Lydia.

"I just came in to try one of your cookies and to introduce myself," he said. His eyes narrowed slightly. "I get the feeling we've already met, though."

"Yes. I'm Lilah Fallon."

He seemed to recognize her name. She felt a sinking sensation. Ever since she had tried to help out with a murder case a few months ago, he had disliked her. She hoped that it wouldn't affect her business at all. Hopefully they could both remain professional.

"Well, if you ever need anything, the police department is only a couple of blocks away," he said. "We like to let all of the small business owners know that we've got their backs."

"Thanks," she said. "I hope I never need you, but it's good to know that you're there."

He nodded and turned to leave.

"Wait," she said. "Didn't you want a cookie?"

"I think I'll pass."

With that, he was gone, leaving Lilah confused and a bit hurt. She had hoped that he might be over his annoyance with her by now, but it seemed that it wasn't so. She tried to tell herself that it didn't matter. She had other things to worry about right now, like Lydia. Why had she acted so strangely when Officer Eldridge came in? Was it just coincidence? Lilah knew that grief could make people act strangely, but the thought of the woman's comment about her husband's life insurance kept coming back to her mind. Was she a suspect in the murder case? Was that why she hadn't wanted to be around the policeman? Lilah knew that she wouldn't get any answers until Lydia came out.

When the widow didn't make an appearance for nearly twenty more minutes, Lilah began to get worried. It was nearly time to close for the day, and she needed to start cleaning up. She knocked softly on the bathroom door during a lull in business, and could barely make out the other woman's reply.

"What?"

"Lydia, it's Lilah," she said. "Is everything all right in there?"

"Is that man gone?"

"Officer Eldridge? Yes, he left a while ago."

The bathroom door creaked slowly open. Lydia peered out. Her eyes were bloodshot, and her makeup was running.

"Are you okay?" Lilah asked.

"I'm fine." The other woman sniffled, then gave a sad laugh. "Well, I'm obviously not fine. I'm sorry. I know I'm a mess. I just wasn't expecting to see him walk in."

"Is there some reason that the two of you don't get along?" She was trying to be tactful; she doubted Lydia would appreciate being asked outright if she was a suspect in her husband's murder case.

"No, no, nothing like that. It's just that he's the officer who first showed up when — when they found John." She took a shuddering breath. "He's the one who told me. Every time I see him, I just flash back to the moment when he told me my husband was dead."

"Oh." Lilah didn't know what to say to that. She felt horrible for the poor woman, but she had no idea how to express it. She was sure Lydia had already heard all of the "I'm sorry's" that she would ever want to hear. "Do you want to sit down in the kitchen and have a cookie?" she said instead. "I have quite a few leftover from today. They were all made fresh this morning."

"Th-thank you. That sounds wonderful," the other woman said.

As Lilah cleaned, she kept an eye on Lydia. She seemed to be doing all right. At least she wasn't crying anymore. That was always an improvement.

As the clock ticked closer to closing time, fewer and fewer customers came through the door. All in all, she was satisfied with how the day had gone. It had been more successful than she had dared to hope. If things kept going this well, she would be able to quit at the diner in no time.

She felt a small pang at the thought of leaving the place for good. While she didn't like coming home smelling like burgers and onions every day, the job had a lot of perks. She liked everyone else that worked there, and knew all the regular customers by name. She could list off their menu in her sleep, and thought she could probably find her way around that kitchen even if she was blind. One of the things that she would miss most would be the flexibility of the job. At the diner, if she had to take a sick day or wanted to switch shifts with someone, it usually wasn't a problem. Here at the Casual Cookie, she would be her own boss, but she also wouldn't have anyone to cover for her if she got sick.

Deciding to worry about things like hiring an employee later, Lilah pushed her worries to the side and tried to focus instead on the fact that the Casual Cookie looked like it was going to be a success. She felt triumphant, and knew that she would probably feel even better tomorrow after catching up on her sleep.

Just minutes before closing, the front door swung open to admit what she hoped would be her last customer of the day. She smiled tiredly and looked up to see Chris Burk standing in the doorway, wearing a Christmas tree sweater and a grin.

CHAPTER FIFTEEN

"**W**elcome to the Casual Cookie," Lilah said. "What can I get you?"

"Oh, let's see… how about a couple of those sugar cookies, a few gingerbread men, and one of those festive chocolate chip cookies." He chuckled. "We keep running into each other, don't we? Funny how that works."

He looked around the store while she packed up his order. He seemed as cheerful as ever. She realized that the lights on the Christmas tree on his sweater actually lit up. She wondered what in the world he did during the eleven months each year when it wasn't December. He seemed like a man who existed purely for the holidays.

"Here you go," she said, handing him the bag. "Will you be paying with cash or card?"

"Cash."

She opened the register and counter out his change. As she was dropping the coins in his hand, Lydia came out of the kitchen.

"Thanks for letting me take some time to…" She trailed off as her gaze fell on the man on the other side of the counter. "Chris. Hi."

"Ms. Lopez."

Lilah was surprised at how cold his voice was. She had already grown used to his perpetually cheery way of speaking.

"That's it?" Lydia said. She sounded angry; another shock for Lilah. The cookie shop owner turned to look at her, wondering what was going on. "This is the third time I've seen you since the accident. You haven't mentioned John once. He was your neighbor. Would it be too much to expect some condolences? I know you never liked him, but this is just going too far."

"I'd say sorry if I meant it," Chris said. "But I'm not. You're better off without that guy anyway. We all are."

"What's that supposed to mean?" Lydia said, her voice rising in pitch almost to a shriek.

Lilah looked between them, at a loss for what to do. She had expected nothing like this. She knew that Lydia was emotional due to her husband's death, but Chris had no excuse as far as she was concerned.

"He was a drunk, and had no respect for anyone," the man said.

"You're just mad that he didn't follow your stupid home owner's association rules." Lydia was crying again. "I don't blame him. They were just Christmas lights. He shouldn't need to put them up if he didn't want to."

"Is this really what all of this is about?" Lilah cut in. "You won't give your condolences over her husband's *death* because of a stupid argument about *Christmas lights?*"

They both fell silent and turned to look at her.

"I moved to that neighborhood because I appreciated the home owner's agreement and expected *everyone* to abide by the rules," Chris said. "Having one dark house on the street every single year? That's not what I signed up for. It just looks bad. Worse, it's right across the street from me. I love the holidays. When I look out my window before bed, I don't want to see dark and gloom. I want to see decorations."

"A man's life is more important than some stupid lights," Lydia said. "Get over yourself, Chris. You'd think that with you being the one who found him, you might show more sympathy than the average person."

Lilah's gasp went unnoticed by both of them. She couldn't believe that she hadn't made the connection before. The news article that she had read the very night of John's death had said his body had been found by a neighbor. Then, a few days later, a neighbor's report had caused Reid's arrest. Could those neighbors have been the same person? Was Chris the one behind Reid's arrest?

"Why would stumbling onto a body in a pool while I was chasing my cat make me more sympathetic? If anything, it just gives me another reason to be mad at him. He wrecked yet another of my days."

"What do you mean, you were chasing your cat?" Lydia asked, her voice quiet now. "I thought you went back there because you saw someone suspicious coming out of the yard."

"Well, yeah, I mean, I saw someone suspicious, but my cat was also back there — that's when I saw them —"

"You told the police you happened to glance out your window and you saw a man slinking around the corner of the house." The other woman's eyes blazed. "Why are you lying now, Chris?"

"I'm not lying. You're the confused one, woman."

"Wait. Stop it, both of you," Lilah snapped. They both turned their angry gazes towards her.

"You've been nothing but nice to me, Lilah, but please stay out of this," Lydia said. "Chris has a lot to answer for."

"I'm sure he does," Lilah said. "Maybe even more than you think."

"What are you talking about?" Chris asked.

"You're the one that made that fake report to the police, aren't you?" she said. "The one about a guy who looked like Reid sneaking around right before John's death."

"Who says that report was fake?" he growled.

"Why would he make a fake report?" Lydia asked, ignoring him. "He wouldn't have anything to gain by it. If he wanted to punish me for not putting a fake reindeer in my yard or something, he could have made the report about me. I know the police already suspected me. They probably would have jumped at the chance to bring me in."

"What if he was just trying to throw them off the trail of the real killer?" Lilah said. "Himself."

The silence that fell was palpable. Lilah, who had been caught up in the moment, suddenly realized that she had just made a terrible mistake. How had she been stupid enough to say her suspicion out loud?

Lydia, who had gone as white as a ghost, turned slowly towards Chris.

"You?" she said in a low voice. "Are you the one who did it?"

Chris glanced between her and Lilah, uncertainty flashing across his face. A moment later, his features hardened as he appeared to come to a decision.

"Yeah," he said. "I did it. I didn't mean to, but I sure don't regret it."

Lydia lunged at him. Lilah didn't know what she was planning on doing, and never found out because Chris simply backhanded her and sent her sprawling across the floor. Holding her hand to her cheek, the woman glared up at him through her tears.

"How could you? So what if he didn't put up our Christmas lights? He was a human being, and he deserved to live."

"He's the one that came at me," Chris said. "It was self-defense. Your lout of a husband was drunk, as usual. My darn cat had gotten out again and made a beeline for your yard. Usually no one's home during the day, so when he came stumbling out of the house towards me, I was caught off guard. He started yelling about me trespassing, and threw a punch. I threw one back. He fell into the pool, smacked his skull against the edge, and went down and didn't come up."

"And you didn't try to save him?" Lydia sobbed. "You could have saved him."

Lilah watched the scene in front of her in horror. The counter was between her and Chris, but she knew it wouldn't be very good protection if he decided to come after her next. Who knew what he would end up doing to her and Lydia. She was certain that he wasn't about to let them go. He would have to know that they would run straight to the police if he did.

"I didn't want to save him. The man was trying to drown himself anyway. I helped him do it, just with pool water instead of whiskey."

Chris pulled his foot back, and Lilah realized what he was about to do an instant before he did it.

"No!" she shouted, and hurled the only thing in arm's reach at his head — her phone. It bounced off and clattered to the floor, but it had served to distract him. The kick that he had been aiming at Lydia missed.

Chris turned towards Lilah slowly, as if he had forgotten that she was there. "You shouldn't have done that," he growled.

He was over the counter in an instant, his hands around her throat. Try as she might, Lilah couldn't break free. She heard Lydia screaming, but the sound was in the background, muted and dimmed by the sound of her own blood pounding in her ears. She clawed as his face, trying to find his eyes, but he seemed to be made of stone. Nothing she did affected him. Her vision was slowly fading, and she felt her hands grow weaker as they tried to push him away.

Suddenly the vise grip around her throat was gone. Lilah was too relieved to be able to breathe again to do anything but massage her neck and take in deep, ragged gasps of air for a few moments. When she finally woke up, she saw someone standing over her and flinched before realizing that it was Reid.

"Are you okay?" he asked.

She nodded mutely and accepted his hand. He pulled her to her feet. She looked over the counter to see Chris lying on the floor. Lydia was huddled in the corner, as far away from him as she could get.

"What happened?" she said, wincing and rubbing her throat once more.

"I knocked him out," Reid said, glancing at his hand. It was already starting to swell. "I guess it's good I took boxing throughout college."

"You got here just in time."

"I would have been here sooner if I hadn't run into Val, Margie, and a woman I'm guessing is your mother in the parking lot." He looked down at Chris. "I guess now isn't the best time to talk about our second date."

In the corner, Lydia gave a relieved sob and started to gather herself up. Lilah looked at the unconscious man on the floor. She was still reeling from the horror of the past few minutes. If it hadn't been for Reid, both she and Lydia might be dead right now. It was a lot to process.

"You sit down," Reid said. "I'll call the police and handle everything."

Lilah couldn't imagine hearing better words. She took a seat next to Lydia and closed her eyes, trusting Reid to pick up the pieces while she tried to wrap her mind around everything that had happened.

CHAPTER SIXTEEN

"**M**erry Christmas!"

Seven glasses clinked in a toast. Margie's table was barely big enough to fit everyone, let alone the mountains of food that were waiting in the kitchen. Lilah was sitting next to her neighbor, with her parents beside her, and Val and her fiancé across from them. Lydia sat further down the table, still looking a bit unsure as to whether she was actually welcome there or not.

"I've got to say, I think this is the first year that Christmas was the least exciting day of the week," Val said when the toast was done. "It's kind of nice."

Life had been hectic since the grand opening of the Casual Cookie on Wednesday, and the subsequent attack. Between running the cookie shop, working at the diner, and giving reports to the police, Lilah had barely had time to breathe. She agreed with Val — it was nice to have a day where she had absolutely nothing she had to do besides help cook, and eat dinner with her friends.

"It certainly was quite the week," Lilah's father said. "I'm just glad that everyone's okay. If only I had gotten her earlier —"

"It wouldn't have changed anything, dear," her mother said gently. "Chances are you would have been with me when the attack happened, and would have been just as useless."

"Still, I would have liked to see that man before they carted him away," her father grumbled. "He attacked my Lilah. No one gets away with that."

"He's not exactly getting away with it," Lilah pointed out. "He's going to jail, after all."

Her close brush with death seemed to have mended her relationship with her father, at least temporarily. She had thoroughly enjoyed showing him around the Casual Cookie, and had been surprised when he seemed to like it. Maybe he wasn't quite as disappointed in her as she had thought.

A knock sounded at the door and she jumped up. "That'll be Reid," she said. "I'll get it."

Her heart lifted when she saw him leaning against the doorframe, a pie in one of his hands. He grinned when he saw her.

"How's dinner going?" he asked.

"We waited for you."

"Two Christmas dinners in one day," he said. "I don't think I'm going to be able to move by this evening."

"How was the meal at your sister's?"

"Delicious, as always. I'm betting Margie's will be just as good, though."

"She's the best cook I know," Lilah said. "It will be scrumptious. Come on in, we're half starved."

"Hold on," he said. "There's one thing I wanted to do first."

He wrapped an arm around her waist and tugged her closer. There was a breathless moment before their lips touched, and then they were kissing.

"I've been wanting to do that for months," he said when they pulled apart.

"Well," Lilah said, trying to corral her thoughts. "I don't think you'll have to wait that long to do it again."

"Come on," he said with a grin, holding an arm out to her. "Let's go inside. Our second date awaits."

Made in the USA
Monee, IL
20 February 2022

91548862R00069